"For all of my family
who keep my days bright.
It's thanks to their love
that you're reading *Starlight*."

~ Jessica M. Vidinha

www.mascotbooks.com

For more information, please contact:
Mascot Books
P.O. Box 220157
Chantilly, VA 20153-0157
info@mascotbooks.com

CPSIA Code: PRT0811A
ISBN: 1-936319-70-5
ISBN-13: 978-1-936319-70-1

Printed in the United States

Starlight

Jessica M. Vidinha

Illustrated by
Amy Donohoe

High above Earth,
past the moon and the sun,
sit thousands of stars,
all smiling but one.
He felt small and dim
surrounded up there
by much bigger stars
with much brighter glare.

"With all of these stars
much greater than me,
from down there on Earth
I'll never be seen.
The people will notice
these big shining spheres
and won't ever know
that I'm even here."

As our little star
looked down below,
he struggled to see
what is our own North Pole.
All of a sudden,
he started to fall
and couldn't believe
his worst luck of all.

"Help me!" he screamed
as he fell from the sky,
"We little stars
do not know how to fly!"
The elves were out working,
Christmas Eve was so soon,
when one elf named May
saw the star and his gloom.

"Quick, everybody,
there's no time to waste,
we've got to catch him
and make sure he's safe."
"Don't even bother"
said an elf in disgust,
"He doesn't look
like any of us."

"That shouldn't matter,"
May said with a grin—
"We should still help him
and then take him in."
She gathered the elves,
some big and some small,
and they all worked together
to stop the star's fall.

"Thank you for saving me,"
he said, looking glum.
"But I don't think
I'm useful to anyone.
Since I'm so tiny
and not easy to see,
the great big sky
will never miss me."

"Why don't you stay here?" asked an elf named Stu. "Santa will find you something to do!"

They brought him to St. Nick,
who was sitting at home,
beside a tall tree
that looked plain and alone.

"Santa," said Stu
with his eyes shining brightly,
"We've got a problem—
and don't take it lightly!
This little star
has come a long way,
and we'd really like it
if you'd let him stay."

After a moment,
Santa knew what to do.
"I think I've got
the perfect job for you!
My tree looks so lonely
without any light;
you can sit on top
and make it look bright!"

The star was so happy—
this lifted his soul.
Even though he was tiny,
he lit up the North Pole.
For years to come,
he'd be a sight to see,
sitting on top of the
Great Christmas Tree.

The End.

About the Author

Jessica was born and still lives in Massachusetts, where she also received her Bachelor's Degree in Writing, Literature, and Publishing from Emerson College. She remembers writing her first story about a cat and a fish at age five. Her favorite picture books were *Fox in Sox* and *A Giraffe and a Half*, as she loved the challenge of reading the silly rhymes out loud. Once she moved on to longer books she loved to stay up late to finish "just one more chapter," to which her mother declared she must be the only parent who had to tell her daughter to put the book away and go to sleep. Jessica hopes this isn't true.

Acknowledgments

I owe my success to anyone who's ever supported me,
but I'd like to thank these people in particular:

— **Mr. Tavares** for assigning the project that led to *Starlight*.

— **Ann** for encouraging me to pursue its publication.

— **Olivia** for assuring me enthusiastically
that a four year old would enjoy this story.

— **Erik** for showing me how to look on the bright side.